W9-AQR-210

01/2014

A Beginning-to-Read Book

What's in the Sky, Dear Dragon?

by Margaret Hillert
Illustrated by David Schimmell

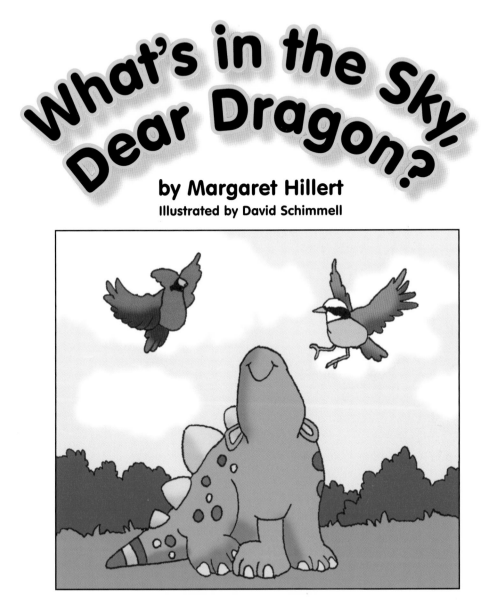

NORWOOD HOUSE PRESS

DEAR CAREGIVER, The *Beginning-to-Read* series is a carefully written collection of classic readers you may remember from your own childhood. Each book features text comprised of common sight words to provide your child ample practice reading the words that appear most frequently in written text. The many additional details in the pictures enhance the story and offer the opportunity for you to help your child expand oral language and develop comprehension.

Begin by reading the story to your child, followed by letting him or her read familiar words and soon your child will be able to read the story independently. At each step of the way, be sure to praise your reader's efforts to build his or her confidence as an independent reader. Discuss the pictures and encourage your child to make connections between the story and his or her own life. At the end of the story, you will find reading activities and a word list that will help your child practice and strengthen beginning reading skills.

Above all, the most important part of the reading experience is to have fun and enjoy it!

Shannon Cannon

Shannon Cannon,
Literacy Consultant

Norwood House Press • P.O. Box 316598 • Chicago, Illinois 60631
For more information about Norwood House Press please visit our website at *www.norwoodhousepress.com* or call 866-565-2900.

LIBRARY OF CONGRESS CATALOGING-IN-PUBLICATION DATA
    Hillert, Margaret.
     What's in the sky, dear dragon? / by Margaret Hillert ; illustrated by
    David Schimmell.
        pages cm. -- (A beginning-to-read book)
        Summary: "A boy and his pet dragon look at both the day and night skies.
    They learn about the sun, moon, animals, and airplanes that move through the
    sky. This title includes reading activities and a word list"-- Provided by publisher.
     ISBN 978-1-59953-580-7 (library edition : alk. paper)
     ISBN 978-1-60357-435-8 (ebook)
    [1. Sky--Fiction. 2. Dragons--Fiction.] I. Schimmell, David, illustrator.
    II. Title. III. Title: What is in the sky, dear dragon?
    PZ7.H558Wg 2013
    [E]--dc23
                              2012043566

Manufactured in the United States of America in Stevens Point, Wisconsin.
243R—092013

What's in the sky, Dear Dragon?
What's in the sky?
We can see some things at night.

Look up. Look up, Father.

Look way, way up.

I see something yellow.
It is pretty. It is big.
It gives us light.

Yes, Yes.
That is the moon.

I see some baby moons, too.

No, no.
They are not moons.
They are stars.
They give us light, too.

Are the little, little ones stars?

No.
They are fireflies.
You can get some to look at,
but then put them back.

Oh, look here.
The owl likes the night sky.

And look at this.
Oh, look at this!

What fun!
What fun!

We will go to bed now.

When we wake up,
we will look at the day sky.

Now what we see is the sun.

The sun is big, big, big.
It gives us light, and helps things grow.

Clouds are in the sky.

Rain is in the sky, too.
Rain is in the dark clouds.

Sometimes the rain and sun
make a rainbow.
A pretty, pretty rainbow.

I see red and orange.
I see yellow and green and blue.

Birds are in the sky, too.
They are pretty too.
Look at them go.

An airplane is in the sky.
It is like a big bird.
It can go away, away, away.
We can go away with it.

We are in the airplane.
We will go, go, go.

You are here with me.
And I am here with you.
It is fun to be in the sky, Dear Dragon.

READING REINFORCEMENT

The following activities support the findings of the National Reading Panel that determined the most effective components for reading instruction are: Phonemic Awareness, Phonics, Vocabulary, Fluency, and Text Comprehension.

Phonemic Awareness: The /s/ sound

Substitution: Ask your child to say the following words without the /**s**/ sound:

sat - /s/ = at	spot - /s/ = pot	Sam - /s/ = am
sand - /s/ = and	she - /s/ = he	said - /s/ = aid
share - /s/ = hare	sin - /s/ = in	stop - /s/ = top

Phonics: The letter Ss

1. Demonstrate how to form the letters **S** and **s** for your child.

2. Have your child practice writing **S** and **s** at least three times each.

3. Ask your child to point to the words in the book that start with the letter **s**.

4. Write down the following words and ask your child to circle the letter **s** in each word:

see	sad	this	sky	say	was
set	clouds	shapes	miss	something	sip
ask	guess	star	said	house	sun